What a Job!

Diane Bair and Pamela Wright

Contents

Rigby

What a Job!

Imagine spending the day helping a pelican with an injured wing. How about taking an hour or two to care for koalas? Or what about spending your time finding loving families for homeless cats and dogs? Some people love animals so much that they choose jobs working with animals.

In this book, you'll meet three people who work with animals. First, there's a man who started a **shelter** for injured birds and other wildlife. Then, you'll see a zookeeper at work. And finally, you'll find out about a woman who works at a shelter for stray dogs and cats.

What does the word *shelter* mean to you?

The Pelican Man

People call Dale Shields the Pelican Man. He began taking care of injured pelicans in 1981. Now, more than 300 **volunteers** help birds and other wildlife at his shelter in Florida. Together, they rescue and give medical care to thousands of animals each year.

"I have been able to communicate with animals since I was a little boy," says the Pelican Man. "Twenty years ago, I had a heart attack. I was very sick. I made a vow that if I lived, I would devote my life to helping animals."

How do you think the Pelican Man learned to help injured animals?

How do pelicans get hurt? Pelicans dive into the water in search of the fish they eat. Fishing boats use the same waters. Sometimes, pelicans get caught in fishing lines and get trapped. Then they can't dive for food. Volunteers from the shelter know how to remove the fishing lines without hurting the pelicans.

The shelter is a busy place. Volunteers answer rescue calls. Rescue trucks arrive throughout the day with new patients. In one room, you might see a **veterinarian** fixing a bat's broken bone. At the same time, a deer that has been struck by a car might be getting stitches. Volunteers clean cages and provide fresh food and water for the animals.

More than half of the animals treated at the shelter get better. They are able to leave the shelter and live outdoors again. About 200 permanently disabled birds live at the shelter.

How did reading this change your mind about working with animals?

Many birds need medical attention.

Koala Keeper and Much More

John Michel works as a zookeeper at the San Diego Zoo in California, but sometimes he feels as if he's in Australia. John takes care of the zoo's Australian animals. This includes wallabies and koalas.

Wallabies are small kangaroos. Some are the size of a rabbit. Some are almost 6 feet long.

John Michel

How do you think John Michel would care for the zoo's Australian animals?

Wallabies live in Australia and nearby islands. They live in forests, grasslands, rocky areas, and swamps.

Koalas are gentle animals. They spend most of their time in trees, much of it sleeping. "When I take a koala from its perch, it holds onto my arm like a tree branch," John says.

People often call them koala bears, but koalas are actually not bears. When koala and wallaby babies are born, they are very tiny. They crawl into a pouch along the front of their mother's body and stay there until they are old enough to survive in the world.

wallaby

As a zookeeper, John spends his day checking on the animals, cleaning their living spaces, and giving them medicine if they need it. He changes their food from time to time and rearranges their living spaces. That way, the animal's life inside the zoo is more like life in the wild, where things change from day to day.

John enjoys sharing what he knows about the animals with kids.

kangaroo

"The best part of my job is getting to know the animals," John says. "As a kid, I brought home lots of animals. I had a spider monkey as a pet." Like many people who work with animals, John loves his work.

spider monkey

How does John Michel care for the zoo's Australian animals? Was your prediction right?

Animal Adoption Manager

Rita Bowes's van can be a noisy one because it is often full of puppies. Rita drives the dogs to the animal shelter where she works. "The puppies like to listen to music as they ride," she says.

Rita is a manager at an animal shelter in Massachusetts. Rita's job is to match dogs and cats with people who will give them a home and lots of love. The shelter is a **temporary** home for puppies and kittens as well as adult dogs and cats. The animals live at the shelter until the shelter workers can find homes for them. Families who would like to **adopt** a pet visit the shelter.

It's important to see how the animals and people get along.

Why do you think Rita would do this job?

Rita says, "We ask the people a lot of questions. We want to make sure our animals go to good, loving homes."

Rita spends a lot of time working with the puppies and dogs at the shelter. She cleans their cages, walks them, feeds them, bathes them, and gives them medicine if they need it.

Why would asking questions help Rita find good homes for the animals?

The animals are looked over from head to tail.

Her favorite part of the job is introducing pets to their new families. "I have a really wonderful job," Rita says. "The best part is helping the animals. It makes me feel like I'm making a difference in the world."

Would you like to work with animals?

Here's what you can do *now* to make it happen:

- Take science classes and try to do well in them.
- Read as much as you can about animal care.
- If you have a pet, spend a lot of time with it.
- Can't have a pet? Offer to be a dog walker for a neighbor.

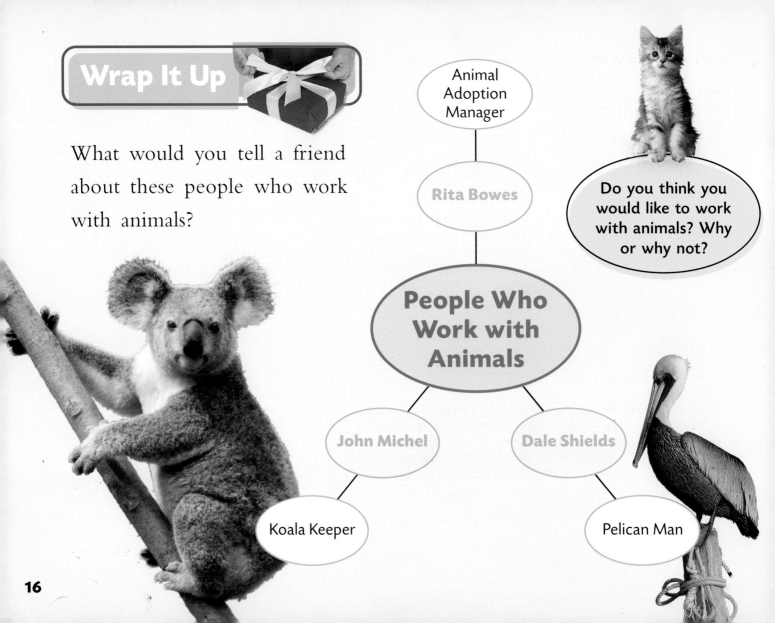

Wrap It Up

What would you tell a friend about these people who work with animals?

Do you think you would like to work with animals? Why or why not?

People Who Work with Animals

Animal Adoption Manager — Rita Bowes

John Michel — Koala Keeper

Dale Shields — Pelican Man